Birth of a Koala

First published in 1986 by
J.M. Dent Pty Limited
34-36 Wadhurst Drive
Boronia, 3155,
Victoria, Australia

National Library of Australia
Cataloguing-in-Publication Data

Burt, Denise
    Birth of a koala
    ISBN 0 86770 038 6.
    I. Koalas — Juvenile literature. I. McLeod, Neil.
    II. Title.

559.2

Typeset by Graphicset,
Mitcham, Melbourne
Printed in Hong Kong.

The producer gratefully acknowledges
permission granted by Roger Martin, B.Sc., M.Sc.,
of Monash University, Melbourne, to use his
transparencies for the illustrations on
Page 20 (A & B), 21 (A), 22 and 24/25.

Produced by Buttercup Books Pty Ltd,
Melbourne, Australia.

Birth of a Koala

Denise Burt

Photographs by
Neil McLeod

J.M. Dent Pty Limited
Melbourne

The koala (Phascolarctos cinereus) is the best known of Australia's many marsupials. The term 'marsupial' means that the female has a pouch in which she shelters her young until they are strong enough to fend for themselves.

Marsupials evolved millions of years ago when dinosaurs were still roaming the earth. At that time, Australia, Africa, South America and Antarctica were all part of one landmass called Gondwanaland. Once the dinosaurs became extinct, the marsupials were able to flourish.

In time, this landmass broke up as a result of the continental drift. Because South America and Australia remained isolated, their fauna survived. The koala was one of the creatures which evolved about this time.

Eventually South America drifted and linked with North America and the more advanced mammals from the North caused the extinction of most of the marsupials in South America. Australia's isolation protected its marsupials and today it has the greatest number of marsupials in the world.

The koala is protected by law, but it was not always so. As recently as the 1920's it was hunted and killed for its thick fur and came very close to being wiped out completely.

Fortunately, it was realised in time that their numbers were down to a few thousand. Surviving koalas were relocated to areas where suitable trees were plentiful and their numbers increased beyond the danger level.

The law now deals very harshly with anyone who kills or injures a koala, or who keeps one in captivity without permission.

The koala is popularly known as a koala bear because of its resemblance to the familiar toy teddy bear. It is really in a genus all on its own. Its closest relative is another Australian marsupial, the wombat, which lives on the ground and eats roots and grasses.

The word 'koala' is an Aboriginal word which had its beginnings in a similar word which meant 'no water'. The Australian aborigines saw that the koala apparently obtains sufficient liquid from the gum leaves which are its natural food source.

Koalas eat the leaves from about twelve species of the eucalypt or gum trees. The Manna Gum is the most favoured in the southern region and in New South Wales it is the Grey Gum. In the northern areas, the River Red Gum and the Forest Gum are the most favoured.

Some feeding takes place in daylight, but the koalas mostly feed in the first two hours after sunset.

In their natural state, koalas are found throughout north-eastern and southern Australia in the coastal regions.

Those in the northern areas are slightly smaller than the southern koalas and their fur is not as thick. This helps them cope with the hotter northern climate.

Koalas in the colder south-eastern regions are stronger and have thicker fur. They have an inner coat of fine thick fur with a longer and shaggier top layer.

The koala's front paws have the 'thumb' and the first 'finger' close together, with the other three making up a second section.

The toes on the hind legs are separated and both front and hind paws have soft padded soles.

Their long, sharp claws are ideal for climbing and holding on to tree trunks and branches.

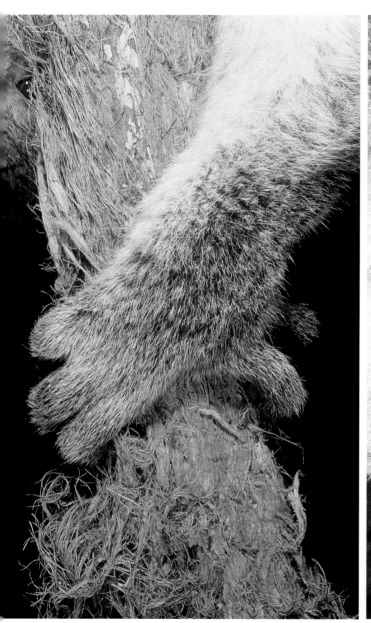
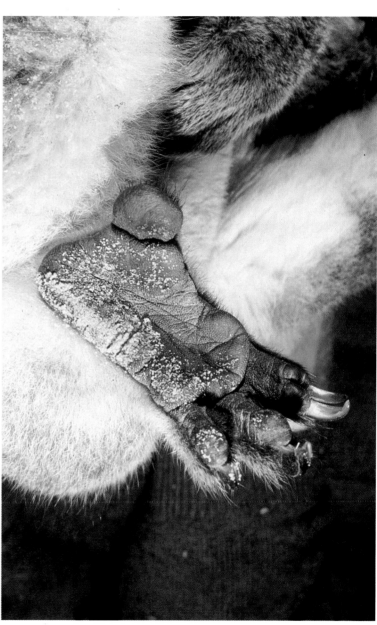

Because the koala is often seen scratching itself, many people think it is trying to rid itself of fleas.

Instead, it is using its long claws to rake through its fur in a form of preening, to fluff out the thick fur.

The koala is a very fussy feeder. It chooses the young leaves at the tip of the branches and eats large quantities.

An adult koala eats about 500 grams (18ozs) of gum leaves every day.

Koalas are very good climbers. They clasp a tree trunk with the sharp claws on the front paws and bring the hind feet up together in a bounding movement.

They are strong swimmers and can survive floods, but each summer a number of these beautiful marsupials are lost as Australia's bushfires take their deadly toll.

Koalas are very agile in the trees, but are clumsy slow movers on the ground. If threatened they move in a leaping sort of run.

The koala can leap from branch to branch and from one tree to another without needing to go down to ground level. It is quicker to stay in the tree tops.

It is also safer.

In its natural habitat, its most common predator is the dingo (the Australian wild dog). In wildlife reserves and parks more koalas are killed by motor cars than by natural predators.

At dusk motorists often fail to see the slow-moving koala on the road.

The female is mature enought to breed in her third year and mates in the warm summer months.

Mating usually takes place at night, high up in the trees and is very difficult to photograph.

The mating call of the male is a deep hoarse grunt, while that of the female is a high-pitched cry. Their courtship can be very noisy as the male warns off all challengers with pig-like grunts and snorts and the female adds her shrill high-pitched calls.

The mating high in the trees continues over several hours and the squeals that accompany it can be confused with the sound of males fighting.

Outside the mating season, the koalas usually behave compatibly, with only occasional snorts from the males to let an approaching male know that he is about to enter 'occupied territory'.

The koala's pouch is different from that of the possum. It opens from the rear and expands upwards and outwards towards the flanks.

Adult male koala

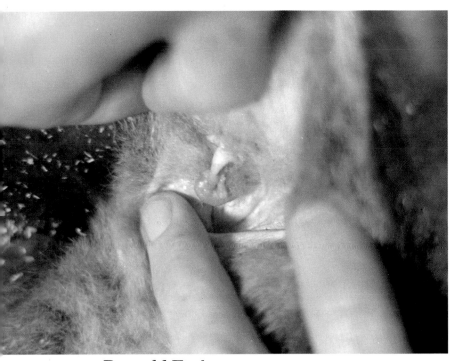

Day-old Embryo

Embryo 10 days old

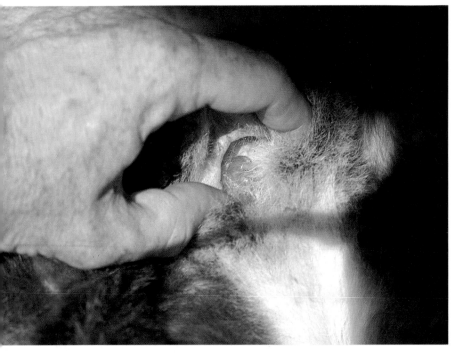

The koala is born after a short gestation period of about 35 days and is only partially developed.

It is blind and hairless and not much bigger than a bean — about 19 mm long (¾″), weighing about .5 gram (a fraction of an ounce).

When it emerges from the birth canal, it wriggles through the mother's fur to reach the pouch.

The mother helps this grub-like creature by licking her fur to provide a 'path' to her pouch.

The pouch is lined with a soft, stretchy membrane and contains two teats.

Once inside the pouch the baby attaches itself to one of the teats.

When it is born, the baby koala has forelimbs which assist it in its journey to the pouch.

The baby remains in the pouch for about six months and, in that time, its thick fur and powerful legs and claws develop.

2 months old

4 months old

The size of the woman's hands holding this baby gives an indication of the koala's size at about five months.

It is well covered with fur and its ears and rubber-like nose are well developed.

As it grows bigger, the baby koala will occasionally pop its head out of the pouch.

At about six months, the baby will climb out of the pouch for short periods.

This allows the mother to clean out her pouch.

The baby is now able to feed on 'pap', which the mother expels from her body, after first having excreted the normal hard pellets.

The 'pap' is soft and fluid and has the strong flavour of the oil from the gum leaves the mother has eaten.

The baby feeds on this for a period of two to six weeks and, in this time, its growth is rapid.

Its first teeth come through and it is now able to nibble some gum leaves.

Female koalas have a strong maternal instinct. There is a very close bond between the mother and baby. For the first twelve months of the baby's life they are rarely apart.

The evidence of this loving bond is one of the reasons why the koala is so appealing.

Although the mother has two teats in her pouch, the birth of twins is not common. In their natural habitat it is difficult for a mother to rear twins. After the babies reach five months, there is not enough room in the mother's pouch for two babies of this size.

Both the babies in this picture survived because the mother was located in a reserve, where a wildlife officer looked after the extra baby.

Koalas are rather solitary creatures. It is more usual to see a mother with her baby, or a single adult koala, than a group.

The males do not help in the rearing of their young. This is left entirely to the mother.

Koalas are very good mothers. The slightest cry of alarm from a young one will bring very swift reaction from the mother.

When the baby emerges from the pouch at about 5½ months it is about 18 centimetres (seven inches) long and is well covered with fur.

It is then carried about by the mother, clinging to her back or hugged closely to her when she is resting.

Even with the baby on her back, the mother can move easily from tree to tree. The baby's strong claws grip the mother's thick fur firmly and ensure a safe ride.

While the mother is feeding on the gum leaves, the baby on her back nibbles and munches on some leaves.

It may not swallow all it munches on but eats enough to get a taste for the leaves.

For the next two or three months the baby will ride on its mother's back during the day, but will return to the pouch at night for warmth.

At about nine months, the koala will leave the mother for short periods, feeding by itself and learning to share its habitat with other bush animals.

Although it is too big for the pouch, it is never far away from the mother.

Sometimes very large babies will try to get back to the 'piggy-back' position, even when they are nearly as big as the mother.

After leaving the pouch, the young koala will stay close to the mother on another branch of the same tree. It will usually stay around until the next mating season when it is likely to be chased off by the male courting its mother.

The 'baby' is really big enough to survive by itself, but it will take up a position in a nearby tree, sometimes with another 'baby' which has also been chased away from another mother.

A koala will finally move off on its own at about twelve months.

Because they eat such a quantity of gum leaves each day, koalas frequently eat themselves 'out of house and home'. When their food supply is threatened, they have to be moved to better feeding grounds.

This involves lassooing the koalas and capturing them in sacks in order to move them safely and carefully, without the rangers being slashed by their sharp claws. The koalas growl and grunt, but they soon settle in their new locations.

Koalas are prone to epidemics. Most of them are caused by a bacteria called Chlamydia, which is responsible for eye diseases and infertility in koalas. In wildlife parks and reserves, where koalas can be studied, investigations of this bacteria are being carried out.

This mother and baby are being cared for by a veterinary officer, who is feeding the baby with an eye-dropper.

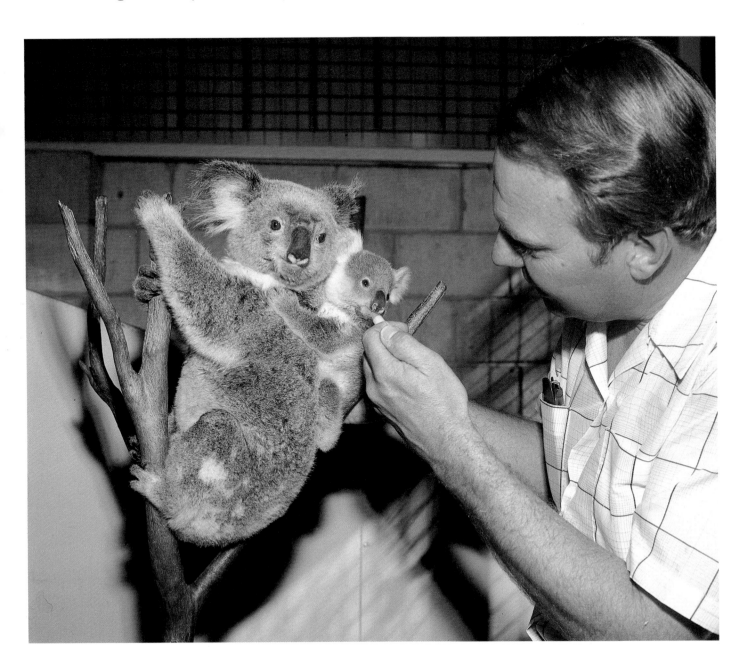

Constant care and protection are necessary to preserve this appealing little marsupial which has become as much a national symbol for Australia as the kangaroo.